Peirene

MARIA BARBAL

TRANSLATED FROM THE CATALAN
BY LAURA McGLOUGHLIN
AND PAUL MITCHELL

Pedra
de
Tartera

AUTHOR

Maria Barbal, born in 1949, is considered by many
to be the most influential living Catalan author. The
clarity with which she presents human relations and
the passage of time has earned her critical acclaim
and a wide readership. She has published eight novels
and has won numerous awards, including the Critics'
Prize, the National Prize for Literature and the Serra
d'Or. She lives in Barcelona.

TRANSLATOR

Laura McGloughlin is a young translator. In 2008 her
translation of Luisa Cunille's three-act play *The Sale*
was published by Parthian.

EDITOR

Paul Mitchell works as a barrister. He has a doctorate
in Persian poetry and was selected to edit this
translation because of his ability to render Conxa's
voice in English.

MEIKE ZIERVOGEL
PEIRENE PRESS

I fell in love with Conxa's narrative voice, its stoic calmness and the complete lack of anger and bitterness. It's a timeless voice, down to earth and full of human contradictory nuances. It's the expression of someone who searches for understanding in a changing world but senses that ultimately there may be no such thing.

First published in English in 2010 by
Peirene Press Limited
17 Cheverton Road
London N19 3BB
www.peirenepress.com

Reprinted 2010

Originally published in Catalan as
PEDRA DE TARTERA
Copyright © Columna Edicions, Llibres I Comunicació. S.A.U., Columna,
Barcelona, 2008, Peu de la Creu, 4, 08001 Barcelona, www.columna.cat

This translation © Laura McGloughlin and Paul Mitchell, 2010

The translation of this work was supported by a grant from the
Institut Ramon Llull

**LLLL institut
ramon llull**
Catalan Language and Culture

Printed in Great Britain by T J International, Padstow, Cornwall

ISBN: 978-0-9562840-1-3

Designed by Sacha Davison Lunt
Photographic image: Skye Chalmers / Photographer's Choice / Getty Images

MARIA BARBAL

TRANSLATED FROM THE CATALAN
BY LAURA McGLOUGHLIN
AND PAUL MITCHELL

Peirene

Stone
in a
Landslide

For my parents

Part One

Anyone could see that there were a lot of us at home. Someone had to go. I was the fifth of six children – Mother used to say I was there because God had wanted me to be there and you have to take what He sends you. The eldest was Maria, who, more than Mother, ran the house. Josep was the son and heir and Joan was going into the church. We three youngest were told a hundred times that we were more of a burden than a blessing. These weren't years of plenty, there were a lot of mouths to feed and not much land, which of course left a hole. So it was decided that I, who was level-headed and even-tempered, would be sent to help my mother's sister, Tia. She'd given up hope of having children but wasn't short of work. She had married a man much older than her who owned land, at least half a dozen cows, poultry and rabbits, as well as a vegetable garden. They got by well enough, but they could do with an extra pair of hands and with the company because they were starting to feel their age. I was thirteen when, with a bundle of clothes in my arms, my father on my left and Maria on my right, I left my family, home, village and mountain. It was just a few kilometres between Ermita and Pallarès, but it meant a day's walk and losing sight of home. At the time, this hurt me more than anything else. As I walked away, I left the only world I had ever known behind.

We walked in silence to the market at Montsent, where my father and Maria were going to pick up some things for home and hand me over to my aunt and uncle. On the way, all that I could think of were the good things about my village. I had never left except to take the animals up the mountain in spring to graze or to sneak off to the *Festa Major* held every year by the four houses which made up the next village. There were a lot of people and not much to eat at those festivals.

I remember the three winters I went to school. Unless you had older sisters to do all the work at home, you didn't go to school if you were a girl. How lucky to be one of the youngest! The teacher made us write in big round letters with little ticks at the end. The *r* started with a curl on the left that I thought looked like a corkscrew. At school we were never cold because Doña Paquita wasn't going to bow to the meanness of our families –

she insisted on a good pile of wood every week for the classroom because she said letters only go in when they're warmed up a little, and if anyone wants you to learn anything then they need to show a bit of good will. She said it in Spanish – *poner un poco de buena voluntad*. The little I know, I learnt in Spanish. I have forgotten most of it. I was amazed the first few times she spoke, this teacher of ours who came from outside. No one understood her. Eventually we did, and she understood us when we talked too, although I don't know why she pretended not to. Maybe she was ashamed of understanding us, or did it out of spite.

I still remember those winter classes as if I was in one this morning. I always sat with Magdalena. Whenever she was supposed to read aloud I couldn't help laughing and Magdalena would stop reading. Doña Paquita would then push back her glasses and glare at me like a sergeant major. I'd get a stomach ache from trying not to laugh when Magdalena started to read again and I'd often feel a little warm drop of pee in my knickers.

I liked going to school. It was special and made me feel being small was good. At home you were just a nuisance. If you played in the haystack, you were making a mess. If you went too close to the fire and clattered the saucepans, you'd caused God knows what kind of calamity. If you picked up

11

a stone or piece of wood to play, you were going to hit someone with it. You were only safe if you were helping to do the milking, peeling potatoes, or carrying firewood. That was being grown-up, but you weren't allowed to have a sip of wine from the *porró* or any bacon after you'd done your work, because for that you weren't grown-up enough.

From the kitchen window the roof of the Sarals' house looked like a high bell tower and the slates sparkled like little mirrors. The rain had stopped and while Mother prepared a thick sheet with ash to do the washing, drops plunged off our roof and hurled themselves at the glass of the window. I watched the channels they made and listened to my mother telling the same story but from a different angle. Tia would have loved to have a daughter like you but God has not granted her wish. And you look more like her than Maria or Nuri, with that long red hair. Don't forget she was the prettiest of us four sisters, and that's why she's made such a good match. You and I, we have the same eyes, like your grandmother's, may she rest in peace, and Tia Encarnació's eyes are very similar too.

But that's not all – here Mother's hands piled the wood to light the fire – they need someone. Who better than one of the family to benefit from this blessing of work…

I couldn't get a single word out even though there was lots I wanted to say. But when she fell silent, I felt a knot in my throat as if a rope around my neck were being pulled from both ends. It began to hurt until the first sob rose in my chest and burst open the knot and then a river of furious tears escaped me, because the last thing I wanted to do was cry. There was no need to say anything. I knew if my mother was spending a morning working quietly at home and talking to me, in no hurry, without interrupting herself all the time with Do this, Where's that? or Have you tidied upstairs yet? it meant this was a solemn occasion. And at home there was little time for solemnity. She brought me a handkerchief and gave me more explanations. They all ended in tears too. Between first my sobs and then hers the scrap of white cotton became a bluish rag, until there was silence. I fixed my eyes on the ground. The fire had started to get hot. It gave me a headache and an irresistible desire to sleep.

The next time I became aware of my mother speaking, she must have been going for a while. As I listened to her, my throat began to tighten again. And so before I choked, I said in a small voice that I would go and live with Tia Encarnació, and when would they come for me? They're going to the market on Monday. Your father and Maria will take you there.

My mother was a woman who knew only two things: how to work and how to save. Maria used to tell us that when our youngest brother Pere was born, my mother was at death's door. That was on the Monday and by the Friday, not even a week later, they couldn't keep her in bed. At thirteen years old I couldn't remember seeing her sit still apart from in a pew at Mass on Sunday.

By the time we got up, she would have been working for ages already or even have gone off to the meadows with my father and Josep. When we went upstairs to bed, she used the time without us to prepare the next day's meal or tidy the house. She was always the last to go to bed and sometimes she'd say a rosary. But for all her devotion, I'm sure she didn't even get to half a mystery. Her tiredness must have held her trapped, like a sparrow in a snare.

She certainly loved us all, but she hardly ever showed it. She didn't have time for all that – she would say that there were more important things that needed her attention first. She didn't know what an idle hour was and was convinced that she had no right to one. When she was old and had time on her hands, she let it slip through her fingers. I think she would rather have died than rested.

There was plenty of work: animals, land and at least seven or eight people to feed. We all helped, but she was the one who put her shoulder to the wheel most to keep it all going. Woman is the heart and soul of the home, she would say.

My father was more talkative, and sometimes he'd say mean things that if you thought them over alone, hurt a bit. On the other hand, he often played with us and put us on his knee and told us stories, most of all in winter when the fire drew us all together after a dinner of vegetables and – when there was some – a sliver of bacon. I remember how we laughed at the story of the old man from Montenar who took the underpants. They were spread out on a bench by the fire to dry. The old man sat down to warm himself. When he got up, a pair of them stuck to his clothes and it was only when he was halfway home, on a freezing cold night, that he realized he had a pair of pants bumping against the back of his legs. He stopped

16

dead on the spot, torn between walking off with them like a thief or going back and ending up frozen stiff like a bird.

But the men in a farming family don't do the worst jobs, and while my father charmed us with his stories, my mother would sit in the firelight darning the holes in a sock for the hundredth time.

Proud and assured, Tia was just as thrifty and hard-working as Mother. But she was also a fiery character who expected to be obeyed.

As I found myself behind the mule, walking quickly because the animal didn't like having a stranger following it and kept trying to get away from me, I so wanted to turn round and run back home as fast as my legs could carry me... Instead I just let my eyes fill with tears, and when I felt them about to fall I took a deep breath and choked them back. I was intimidated by my uncle sitting stiffly on top of the mule and I didn't want him to hear me even sigh. I kept telling myself that they were doing me a favour and I was doing my family a favour too. One less mouth to feed every day... Oncle had picked up my bundle of clothes and carried it in front of him on the animal's neck. He seemed preoccupied and he'd hardly said a word to me. I didn't dare tell him that my sandals were causing me blisters. They were Maria's new ones that she'd given me before leaving home so I'd be better turned out, but she had bigger feet than me. Now they rubbed against my skin and where it rubbed it burnt painfully. I wanted to get to Pallarès as soon as possible to end the ordeal. The mule's tail moved rhythmically. When the flies landed on it, he would flick it upwards, straight away let it drop and then start again. Just when I had lost all hope of ever arriving, Oncle announced: We're nearly there. For the first time that day, a great joy rushed through me and I realized what a fool I'd been to be so afraid the whole journey, as if I were just another cow on the way to market to be sold. But it wasn't like that. I wanted to hug Tia, who hadn't come to the market at Montsent. After all, it was she who was my mother's sister and I had no real connection with my uncle, because he wasn't from our family.

I don't know why I'd imagined they lived outside town. I realized I was wrong when Oncle turned down the street between the houses to the plaza. I felt my cheeks burn as people greeted him and looked at me. When we were in front of my new home and he had got off the mule, some women who had been sitting gossiping amid a group of screaming children came closer to look and ask questions.

Ramon, what a lovely girl you've found at market. We thought you didn't know enough about girls to pick one out... She's our niece from Ermita. She's spending the winter with us.

I didn't know where to look, everyone had their eyes fixed on me and I just stood there, my head spinning and foggy from thinking so much. I felt my legs wouldn't carry me, and the sweat stung my thighs. Then Tia saved me. She broke up the circle of people and held me tightly. The world seemed to dissolve in front of me. Her tenderness surprised me and broke down the whole wall of reasoning I'd built against sadness. She grabbed me round the waist and almost swept me off my feet, carrying me upstairs away from all the people.

She didn't say anything until she got me to the kitchen. We went down a long, dark corridor and only when she sat me on the bench, did I hear her ask the question: Why are you crying?

My aunt and uncle's house was very big. Almost as big as my parents' at Ermita. Many years ago it must have been a house full of people and hustle and bustle because it had a ground floor, two storeys and then a loft under the roof.

The stable and the threshing yard took up the whole ground floor at street level, and you could go out onto the plaza through a big gate. Stairs opposite the gate led up to the first floor, where there was a small hall leading to more stairs straight ahead and an uneven corridor on the right. On one side, the corridor led to a closed room and, on the other, to a big sitting room dominated by an open fire with a blackened chimney. It also had a small stone sink and a long table with two benches. From the room with the fireplace you could go down to the cellar, which took up a tiny corner of the cowshed. The closed room was used as a dining room on festivals and holidays.

Behind the sitting room, which served as a kitchen and dining room, was the haycock. From there you could drop the hay directly into the animals' troughs through some grilles in the floor. You had to know where the holes were or your leg would sink down through the hay right next to a cow's head. Beside the haycock was a cage which looked like a real little house – the rabbit hutch. Half a dozen baby rabbits and their mother had plenty of space to move around inside. When I used to feed them, I only had to bend my neck because I easily fitted inside.

The second floor had four bedrooms, each with its own big iron bed, a washbowl and a jug. In the two largest there was a window and also a little wardrobe cut into the wall, with shelves. From this floor stairs led to the loft. Up there, a strange thing happened. Even though it was the highest place in the house, the river sounded as if it ran just outside. There was a small window up very high and when you leaned out, you could hear the rushing of the water as if it were close enough to touch, but in fact there was a terrifying long drop down.

From the first day the loft was one of my favourite places in the house. There were sieves, baskets and tools lying around, and one evening I discovered a trunk full of dresses from when Tia was young or perhaps even older, from Oncle's family. They were worn and crumpled, but whenever I was sent to find something up there I couldn't stop myself opening the trunk and putting one on over my apron. They made me dream of other times. Sometimes I was tempted to tell Tia, to see if she would make over one of the dresses for me, but I didn't dare. It would show I'd been poking my nose where I had no right to be and I felt myself blush even at the thought of it.

The meadow I liked best was Tres Aigües, where three streams met. On one side ran the Arlet, bathing the meadow before it left its deposit in the river. Its lower boundary was marked by the Orri itself, and along the top was the irrigation channel from the Torna spring. The grass there grew good and tall and it was the only place you could harvest three times: the first as usual, but then twice more after reaping. It wasn't a very large meadow, and while we worked we could see each other. For me, this was one of its charms because in the two Costa Varada meadows, you could look up and find that suddenly you were all alone. I knew that the others were behind the slope or the row of hazel trees, but a feeling of being completely alone would grip me and I'd start to remember the hundreds of terrifying stories I'd heard about vipers and all kinds of snakes. I could hardly work because I was afraid of what I might find in the grass I was turning... if it weren't for the thought of Oncle making fun of me I'd have gone to find the barrel and have some water. I was completely alert as I raked and didn't miss even the smallest movement in the grass. It was only when I caught sight of Tia's dark scarf that I felt safe again.

We'd spent the afternoon turning the grass in Tres Aigües. It was getting dark. The breeze made a restless sound through the nearby hazel trees. I heard Oncle's whistle and I picked up my rake and pitchfork. I was hot under my headscarf and felt the sweat burning the roots of my hair. When I took the scarf off I heard all sorts of sounds, above all the noise of the flies. I ran to the cart as fast as I could but waited for Tia before I got in as she had stayed to close the gate. While I stood there, I looked at the land divided up into small irregular plots. I thought, even the richest man here is still very poor. The plots gave at most four cartloads of hay. The mule seemed to be looking at me with his peaceful gaze, and I rubbed his nose with my hand.

The bell tower appeared, stretching its neck over the houses of Pallarès. As we went down towards home, the stones made the wheels bounce so much we nearly fell out.

Tia and I sat right at the back of the cart. I could smell the grass, welcoming and soft. She told me that the parish had asked for me to pass the plate of basil on the day of the *Festa Major*. Of course you will go, we will get a dress of some sort, she added before I had a chance to open my mouth. Even in the bumping and bouncing cart, I could feel myself trembling. It was happiness.

I closed my eyes and those first days of my new life seemed very far away: the nights I cried myself to sleep remembering each and every person from home, the times I would wake with a start, and the anxiety that didn't leave me all day. How quickly I'd got used to such a great change! But if I counted it up, I'd already been away for half a year. And now I felt, not fully, but almost as if I'd been born in Tia's house.

When you knew Tia well, you came to love her, because she didn't begrudge what she gave you as long as you followed her orders to the letter. Decide, then act, that was her, and she didn't like to be contradicted. Like my mother, she was not demonstrative, but in her own way she showed affection. A glass of fresh milk, still warm from the cow, beside my plate, without a word. I knew they saved it for the calves, or if there was more than enough, they took a few litres to the Augusts' to earn a peseta or two.

Oncle kept quiet, like that first day on top of the mule, but he wasn't bad-tempered. I wore myself out helping him. He worked and worked. I learnt to do everything, outside the house as well as in. Exactly as they had shown me, without any touches of my own which they might think showed a lack of respect.

They liked everything: the chorizo and the black pudding, the cuts of ham. They even liked the bacon. It's much tastier than the stuff down there, they would say.

I enjoyed seeing how they kept helping themselves to more and the way they used their knives for almost everything. Tia's cousin even cut the tiny bit of fat off the ham and left it at the edge of his plate. They eat like kings, Oncle would say. When I took the plates out to the kitchen, I picked it up with two fingers and ate it – the fat I mean. I'd always liked that intense flavour, even more than the lean, and besides, they'd taught me not to waste anything.

City people are different. They're a bit picky about food and so they put on airs. As soon as they start working behind a counter, their heads get swollen. That's what my aunt and uncle said, and I believed every word of it, but I liked the cousins from Barcelona coming up every year. I enjoyed how they filled the house and embraced Oncle and Tia, wiping away the tears and saying, This young lady gets lovelier every time, and what beautiful curly hair! In Pallarès no one says "young lady" nor "lovely". I understood these words even if I didn't use them and they pleased me, and I thought that a language is like a tool that each person picks up in their own way, even if it is used for the same purpose.

They certainly made extra work for us. Sometimes Tia would nearly burst because she wanted everything to be nice, but she also had to tend to the animals and the meadows as well as the kitchen and there weren't enough hands to do it all. It was because of these visits that I began to cook and Tia became more relaxed. At first she tasted everything and she didn't trust me at all, but gradually she saw that I had sense and patience and she let me prepare the salads on my own. After that, the omelettes and vegetables, later the stews, and last of all, the soup. For my aunt and uncle, soup was sacred, and it was the badge of their trust in me when they at last let me make it. We had soup every day. Like bread, you had to have it.

When the cousins from Barcelona came, we would spend a lot more, but they would also bring coffee, a box of biscuits and a slab of chocolate, which we loved best of all. I remember one year they brought a porcelain fruit-stand which certainly looked worth whatever they must have paid for it. It had a pretty basket with a plaited handle and an edge contoured in waves to hold the fruit better. There was a porcelain ribbon round the outside, painted with round blobs which were cherries, a stalk and two leaves on each one. Tia always moaned about that present. It'll break if you even touch it and then you'll never be able to fix it – fruit is meant to be kept somewhere cool, not piled up to look nice, and so on and so forth. I saw that the cousins had given it with good intentions and that was what mattered. It was also true that I loved pretty things, but I kept quiet because I didn't want to make my aunt and uncle angry, especially not Tia, who was so practical. Better a piece of stale bread, she'd say, than something that just looks nice.

I know now that the happiest period of my life began about then, even if, truth be told, the bad times were just waiting behind all the laughter.

Very few festivals were celebrated in those years. There was so much work! Sundays were different because we started the day outdoors later, after we went to six o'clock Mass. And that was just the women, since Oncle and most of the men of the village didn't go. The only ones who did were the old men at the head of the two most important families in the village, the Augusts and the Sebastiàs. From our pew, which was in the last few rows on the right-hand side, I could see almost everyone. Silent, a little shrunken in the cold. The women were like little trees covered in thick black veils. You left with a hurried greeting, and then it was quickly back home to gather tools or light the fire, depending on the time of year and who was at home.

The best festival by far was the one in the summer: the *Festa Major*! It was on a Sunday to save time and came towards the end of the really hard work in the meadows. The harvesting and threshing would all have been done days before and if the weather hadn't been bad the hay would be gathered in. All that was usually left was the second harvest.

The plaza was decorated with coloured paper bunting but it had to be washed down and swept a number of times throughout the day because the cows still had to go out to graze and they left it covered in dung before the solemn Mass. On the day of the festival, Mass was at ten o'clock, then again at the hour of the procession, and once more before the dance.

It had taken a long time for the other young people of the village to think of me as truly from there and not as a stranger. That was why they didn't ask me to carry the plate of basil at the end of mass until I was sixteen. Being asked meant being one of them and helping with all the preparation for the *Festa*: from searching for musicians to cutting up the cake which was offered from another plate at the same time as the bouquets of basil.

I don't know if my shyness came from my nature, my age or just from the bad luck of not being the daughter of the house where I lived.

I felt I didn't belong there and I only dared walk around on tiptoes. I believe I was finally accepted for two reasons: a word from Tia to the parish priest, and, although I don't like to say it, because it was rumoured that I was brighter than most of the local girls who were in line to inherit. Just hearing that people thought this made me blush to the roots of my hair, and when I left the house the day after I found out, I was convinced that everyone looked at me differently and was spying on me from behind their shutters. I felt more false than ever, as if I had committed a grave sin that no one would forgive me for. Now, at the distance of so many years, I don't think my instinct was wrong, even though I was very soon to overcome my fears and my timidity. My life was about to change again, enormously. That winter I got to know Jaume.

Time passed and no one spoke of home. Of my family. In five years I had seen Mother and Maria only once, when they came for the *Festa Major* during my first year in Pallarès. Another time we met my father and Josep at Montsent fair. There I learnt that my brother Joan had left the seminary, a long time before he was able to say Mass. The roads were long and everyone was needed at home.

My aunt and uncle said nothing about going back and I didn't dare mention it. Was I happy there? I had no idea. I'd lived with my heart in my mouth a bit, worried about what they might throw back in my face. Maybe the poverty of my family... But I'd got used to them and their way of doing things. And it's true, the thought of leaving Pallarès to return to Ermita became stranger every day.

Everyone else must have been thinking the same thing. And why not see me as a potential match, since the land, the house, the vegetable garden and the four animals could one day be mine?

Martí, the younger son of the Sebastiàs – the second most important family in the village – started hanging around me. I knew nothing of life, but Tia wasn't against it. Straighten that apron, girl, boys notice everything! I felt ill at ease and didn't open my mouth. Martí wasn't much for conversation either. He didn't really walk next to me, he just followed and stared at me as if he was about to say something important. People said that his family were brutes who shouted a lot and resorted to their fists if necessary. I felt, I don't know, more fear than happiness. But no one had ever asked me what I wanted, and I didn't know how to say no. So, I just did everything to avoid meeting him, even changing the times I went to the fountain and the vegetable garden.

I'd made friends with Delina Arnau because we shepherded the animals in the Solau meadows together. Her parents had the one next to ours. While the animals were grazing she explained a lot of things to me. You could say I got to know the whole village just by talking to her, house by house and person by person. It seemed almost impossible that she could know so much without ever setting foot inside the houses! She was a brave and happy girl with nothing to hide, and I was often spared from having to be with Martí by spending my time with her. Send him packing, she would tell me, and I'd laugh at her decisiveness. What should I say to him? Say that you already have a fiancé in your village. I didn't know how to tell such a big lie, but I thought if he got too much then that's what I would tell him.

It wasn't necessary. That Monday I went down to market with Oncle. We needed to buy something for the house and Tia sent me. When it was time to go back, Oncle said we had a lift from the blacksmith at Sarri. I was glad not to have to do that walk! When I got up onto the cart, my heart leapt into my mouth when I saw a bright smile and heard a voice say: How are the people of Pallarès? It was a young man, maybe the blacksmith's son, who was making room for me. He was shorter than he appeared at first glance because he was very slim. Dark chestnut hair, a little bit wavy and combed with a side parting, wide forehead and small but lively eyes under finely-drawn eyebrows. A mouth that wasn't too big but was always about to laugh, so much so that if he wasn't smiling, the seriousness of his face was striking.

Oncle preferred to sit beside the driver in case he had to help lead the animals. At first I didn't dare lift my eyes from my feet, almost hidden under my skirts, but soon I was laughing as I listened to Jaume. He was so open and full of charm that I quickly forgot my shyness. Even so, for the whole journey I couldn't hold his gaze when he looked me in the eye.

I don't know why people called me Conxa. Really my name was Concepció, but since they had to call us so often as children I suppose that was too long. That's how it started. No one else in the family was called that, even though Assumpció, Encarnació, Trinitat and Concepció were very common names. I became Conxa, and even now I don't know who began calling me that instead of Concepció. Still, the reason was clear: Conxa was shorter. I was convinced that a Conxa would be fat and beefy and, since I was so thin, when people asked my name I always thought they would burst out laughing and I'd feel bad. But Jaume told me that saying my name was like eating a sweet, that it was the name of something small and delicious that he liked very much. It was as if he'd been born to take away my fears, to bring light where I saw darkness and to flatten what felt like a mountain to me.

It wasn't long before I saw him again, but by then between my aunt and uncle and Delina I'd heard the whole story, chapter and verse. All about him and his family. He was indeed from the Sarri blacksmith's family. He was the second son and he had an older brother who was the heir, married with children. Jaume couldn't make a living off the land as it was all going to the heir, and so he'd learnt a trade. Or more accurately, two trades. He was a builder and carpenter, and he worked here and there wherever a house needed to be built or repaired. They even said he'd been to the Aran valley. They knew him to be hard-working and quick-witted but, because of the nature of his work, he appeared to be a drifter and freer than most men, who only looked at the ground to work it or to the sky to figure out what the weather will bring. I realized that they saw him as an outsider, someone who'd managed to earn himself a living, but this had more or less divided him from his family. If only he'd learnt to be a blacksmith like his grandfather! I heard them say. All this left me with a heavy heart. I almost felt ill and decided not to think about that journey with him, this man who'd put new colours into my mundane world.

But he came back that same Thursday, about the time the sun burst into the plaza, and we went outside to take advantage of the good weather with sheets to darn or to make stockings. He was a very good storyteller. The moment we let him speak, we all stopped working, Tia, Delina, the young Melis girl and me. I was worried that he would hear my heart thumping over all the laughter, and that my cheeks would betray me. Before he left, he asked if we could dance together in Pallarès. He wanted to dance and Sarri was quiet as a grave.

Delina said to him, How unusual that you've stayed this long in your village. Before he answered, he looked at me and then replied that at the moment he was repairing his father's house and had several more days' work to go. Until Christmas, perhaps.

Tia showed me a dress of hers which I could make over if I wanted, but I would have to sort it out myself. Darning she could do well, but anything much finer, no. I got over my embarrassment and went to the Esquirols', where they needed people. They said that Toneta had silver fingers. With her help I managed to do it. In exchange I would go there the day they slaughtered the pigs, to help them make sausage. I used every daylight hour and, once the dress was taken in, lengthening it a little wasn't too difficult. So there would be no sign of it, I made a little trim from the offcuts. Buttoned from torso to the neck, it was dark green with a sash, and a wide skirt down to my feet.

I thought it would never come, but at last the day of the dance arrived. I trembled as I went down the stairs of our house, even though Delina was with me. By the time we entered the schoolroom, with the tables all pushed against the walls, the music had already started up. I was surprised by the way people looked at us as we came in. The Augusts were there, so were the Sebastiàs… as if they were in charge of everything. Jaume wasn't there and I didn't know how to say no. Soon I was dancing up and down with Martí Sebastià. He was as fat as a pig. I looked at his temples dripping with sweat and his bright, strange eyes. His hand grasped me closer to his body at every turn. I could hardly breathe and felt almost suffocated. I tried very hard to keep him at a distance, this great barrel that might roll onto me and crush me into the ground with his immense weight.

I could see that I wouldn't get away from my partner easily. But as soon as he arrived, Jaume made it so simple by laughing as if we'd always known each other and saying: Now it's the turn of the boys from Sarri to dance with the girls of Pallarès! Martí was taken aback but didn't have time to answer because I was already spinning around the room with Jaume. His face was so sour that I didn't dare look at him standing there rooted to the spot.

We didn't stop dancing all night. The wind whistled outside and it must have been very cold but the back of my neck was drenched in sweat. When I saw that Old Tonet was packing up his accordion, I stopped. I could hardly breathe. The night was black as pitch and I felt that some kind of miracle had happened. It touched my eyes, my lips... Only when I felt the icy air outside did I wake up and then, as if it was any old thing, he said if I wasn't against the idea I should tell my family that he wanted to marry me and that he would return on Sunday evening to find out the answer.

It was six steps from the schoolroom to the door of my home. The walls touched to form one of the corners of the plaza. I was in front of the steps that I'd come down a few hours ago and I didn't recognize myself. I wanted to force myself to believe that I was the Conxa who'd come to Pallarès to live with my aunt and uncle. But that meant nothing to me. Now I could only be Jaume's Conxa. The mad joy that I felt didn't make me run around though. Instead I was very still, unable to move from the bottom step where we said goodbye, however much the freezing handrail made me want to go up the stairs.

All I longed for was to go a few moments or half an hour or so back in time, to remember. And feel his presence at my side again. I could still hear people talking nearby and instinctively I raised my head. Jaume smiled at me from the other end of the plaza and waved goodbye. Then I ran as fast as my legs could carry me up the steps. I didn't feel part of this world: it felt as if I was dreaming.

Part Two

The tears I cried because they wouldn't let me marry Jaume became a distant memory. In the end good sense had won out. There was no reason for us not to marry. But behind the few words spoken on the matter, my aunt and uncle had taken a lot of things into account.

The chance of making a better match with Martí Sebastià or others, the fact they were my guardians, Jaume's humble position as a tradesman...

But everyone knew that at the Sebastiàs there was a lot of land and little inclination to work: the father was an idiot, the mother was bossy and as for the son, he didn't like to lift a finger. We've already talked about the son. He was a bewildered boy, always clutching his mother's skirts like a little child. And besides all that, they ate like pigs. It would take a very particular young woman to fit into their house. My aunt and uncle understood this. And there was another thing in our favour: I was their ward and would inherit from them, and because Jaume wasn't going to inherit any land, he could come to live in Pallarès. At first it was a problem that he wasn't fully devoted to the land, but he got round this by promising my aunt and uncle that he would help with the heavy summer work – the harvesting, reaping and threshing – but would be a builder in the winter, wherever there was work for him. They would take charge of the money he earned and he would also fix up the whole house, which was badly in need of repair.

As tempers cooled, what had looked like a bad deal at first gradually began to seem more attractive to my aunt and uncle. I think promising to let them handle the money made up their minds. At that time, there was hardly any money in the villages. It was only ever seen when livestock was sold.

I don't mean to say that it was a purely commercial arrangement, because I know that my unhappiness and silence after the initial refusal helped to calm the storm. Tia had not married a man much older than her in vain and she must have been sensitive to the love between two young people. Maybe she was cleverer than she let on and could see that with my spirits so low I was capable of going along with Jaume's desire to set up home on our own.

But I felt bound by gratitude to my aunt and uncle, especially to Tia. Oncle was a shrewd man, who didn't say much, good or bad, a man of routine, who seemed content to live with his wife's lively, enterprising spirit. He left most things to her except overseeing the work in the fields and trading livestock. He was a man of few friends and relations and because he was a hard worker and not in the least conceited, equally had no enemies.

Tia had been almost entirely responsible for everything to do with me and the thought of leaving made me feel guilty. Perhaps deep down I was afraid of losing what I'd learnt to own. Jaume accepted my inability to feel free and he tied himself, with me, to the land and two people who were used to doing as they pleased. But it is fair to say that in those days love made up for any sense of being tied down.

The heat had come again. It was June 1921. The meadows were golden and the poppies were in full bloom. The buzzing of flies looking for food could be heard everywhere. The wild hazel and walnut trees were turning green near the river, like the poplars. The mountain was an ants' nest of workers moving between yellow and green, of carts on the earthen tracks and of the whistles of tools hacking mercilessly into slender stalks. The earth was becoming spongy from the stream that had to last it a whole year. Only the squeak of the cork from the jug or the barrel raised the farmers' eyes to the sky briefly.

Mowing left me tired, but I would run home through the meadows with my breasts leaking inside my blouse to feed Elvira. It nearly killed me. I would always be anxious as I ran – she must be crying, I thought – even though if I was late, I knew Tia would give her a bit of bread dipped in milk. But she wanted only her mother – everyone said she cried to be with me, not because she was hungry. She had so little of me in her first summer. So many hours had to be spent working outdoors! Jaume sometimes signalled to me to go home and I did, but I was afraid that Oncle might notice and grumble. And so I went from one place to the other like a fugitive, from Elvira to work and work to Elvira. Looking back now, I see that there was a lot of toing and froing. But Jaume's constant support gave me strength and pushed me towards the most important thing: our daughter. He would say: people are more important than anything else. I needed help to see this because I had been taught the opposite. When the land and animals were taken care of, *then* you turned to people.

Jaume was impatient with routine and old habits, but he was careful to steer clear of quarrelling with my aunt and uncle. We'd endured enough before marrying. The desire to avoid scenes made us treat them with greater respect, even if sometimes we had to bite our tongues. I was grateful that Jaume behaved like this. And he was quick to smile and say he was the happiest he'd ever been, happy to be young, in love and a father.

Elvira was born just days before our first anniversary. It was the 18th of November and Jaume had a job in Montsent. As she was born on a Tuesday, he didn't know about it until Anton

Peret went there on Friday. He left everything immediately and as night fell he came up on foot through the snow which had frozen on the roads. No one expected him until Sunday.

How happy it made me to see his red face appear from under his muffler hours after night had fallen! He hugged me tightly, then went straight to look at the little girl sleeping in the cradle nearby. He didn't say a word but came close to me again and took my hands. The contrast between warm and cold soon disappeared. For a time we couldn't say anything. I told him all about the birth, though in quite a muddle and with a few tears. He found it strange that he'd lived three days without knowing he had a daughter in the world. He felt a bit cheated. After a while he kissed me and left promising to drink a bowl of warm milk. He wouldn't allow me to get up and prepare it for him. He walked back to Montsent all night in time to be at work at daybreak.

When I told Tia about this the next day, her face was unmoved but her eyes betrayed her. I think it was then that Jaume began to win her over, but in secret.

The days were flying by. I still hadn't learnt what it meant to be a mother with Elvira at one year old and I'd already noticed my belly showing the second child was on the way. Maybe this time it would be a boy. I don't know why that was what everyone worried about most. An heir. And I didn't know if I wanted a boy because the general feeling was better a boy than a girl, or if I just wanted one. To have a girl and a boy, one of each.

A boy will be a man. And a man has the strength to deal with the land, the animals, to build. But I didn't see it so clearly. When I thought about the families I knew well, I saw the woman as the foundation stone. If I thought about my home, it was my mother who did all the work or organized others to do it. Not to mention Tia. The woman had the children, raised them, harvested, took care of the pigsty, the chicken coop, the rabbits. She did the housework and so many other things: the vegetable garden, the jams, the sausages... What did the man do? Spent the day doing things outside. When a cow had to be sold. When someone had to be hired for the harvest. It wasn't obvious that the man did more or was more, but everyone said, What is a farm without a man? And I thought, What is a house without a woman? But what everyone had always said weighed on me. I only knew that I wanted a boy.

It was certainly more difficult doing everything pregnant. Jaume helped me a lot, but he was away a lot, too. In the winter, whole weeks at a time. Elvira and I – she in particular – lived between the joy of seeing him every Saturday and the sadness of seeing him leave every Monday. Since he spent

49

so much time away, he knew many people. Often at home I saw him looking absent, and when I asked him what he was thinking about, I was disappointed to learn that it wasn't me or Elvira or the new baby about to arrive. He would say: Nothing, or I was thinking of this or that house in Montsent or Sarri where they need such and such done and how little it would cost them to do it if... then he would look at me and stop talking, stroke my hair as if I were a little girl and decide that there was something he needed to do. Just having him present wasn't enough for me. I wanted satisfaction, to work out his secrets and all that I believed he only half explained, but there was no time for us to be alone. There was always some work to be done, there was always someone to see. Maybe he didn't feel this way, but I didn't dare ask him in case he laughed at my worries as silly.

Sometimes I spoke to Delina about it. Our friendship continued despite the fact that her parents had fallen out with my aunt and uncle about when to water the Fontnova vegetable garden. Delina saw things very differently to me. She believed that all men are the same, that when they have a wife safe and secure at home, they forget her. That the illusion of love only lasts two days and there's no need to make it more complicated. I didn't see it like that, but I didn't know how to explain myself, how to argue against her. I only wondered how she could be so sure of herself if she didn't even have a sweetheart. She seemed to hold a grudge against men because they hadn't realized what she was: a woman from head to toe, clever, hard-working and more or less as poor as everyone else. She had a point.

But with me, Jaume had made me somebody, and I felt gratitude mixed in with my love for him. Other people often annoyed me, even the children sometimes. Work, yes, it made me feel alive, stopped me complaining and left me unable to think. But when Elvira awoke crying in the night and I'd calmed her, I couldn't go back to sleep. I would lie thinking, going from my earliest memories as a child in Ermita to Jaume's face smiling at me for the first time in Montsent from his father's cart, with the following day's work passing in and out of my thoughts, muddled and messy. And just when I felt I was dropping off, Tia would wake me, surprised that I hadn't yet lit the fire.

Our neighbours on one side were the strangest people in the village. The family was made up of a father, more or less Oncle's age, two daughters and a son-in-law. Soledat was already middle-aged, and Tereseta had married poor Lluís two winters before Jaume and I got married. The mother had long since died, before I came to live with my aunt and uncle. Her name was Trinitat, and while she was alive her husband was as timid as a mouse. People said that she had been a woman of few words and it was even rumoured that she was a witch. She never went outside and she was only ever glimpsed spying from a corner of one of the windows, or from the open balcony when the weather was fine. People were afraid of her, but in desperate cases they'd ask her advice. She would recommend potions and say prayers. Those who had been up the very long staircase to the first floor didn't want to say anything when they came back out. A good friend of Tia's had told her that it was as dirty as a farmyard up there – dried herbs hanging everywhere, and when she left she'd seen a raven's claw stuck to the door that made her blood run cold.

But once Trinitat was dead, the husband began to tell all the people who had nothing to do in the plaza, the old people like him and the children, that his daughters, starting with the eldest, had a claim to the throne of England. You can imagine how this news spread through the village, completely mixed-up, because to begin with few people had the faintest idea where he meant. Instead of accepting that he was mad, his daughters followed their father in everything he did and became furious when children openly mocked Soledat as Queen Soledat. Tereseta, who was one step further away from the crown than her sister, didn't become quite so angry but tried to set her husband on Soledat's tormentors, shouting herself hoarse from the street for him to come. This provoked even more riotous mocking. Poor Lluís would suddenly become as deaf as a post and when his father-in-law went out into the street, he would find himself a job far away in the sty or vegetable garden. Then he would come back late for dinner that day too. Not a soul would have denied that he was the hardest-working man in the whole village.

What is certain is that Soledat scared the children and more than once nearly managed to knock one down when she was chasing them. She must have been nearly forty, tall and skinny, with her hair pulled back into a little bun right on top of her head. Her sunburnt face was creased with many wrinkles and she had two small eyes which were constantly alert. When autumn came, she would put on a black scarf which covered her hair and part of her forehead. Nothing in the world would make her take it off until it was summer again. Both she and Tereseta were sullen women who had nothing to do with anybody except to start disputes that ended in a lifelong enmity. When they dug their heels in, no one could budge them.

I was going heavily up the steps with a bundle of grass for the rabbits. Soledat noticed me from the balcony and saw that I was pregnant. I had to listen as she said, Again, already? and that Jaume and I were very busy workers, with a laugh that made the blood rise to my cheeks. And then, fixing me with her magpie eyes as if she were looking inside me, she told me in pained terms: It will be another girl.

She arrived along with the spring of 1923. It was the last day of March, when the ground was still frozen every morning. We called her Angeleta.

Apart from the elder sister's jealousy of the younger, the next six years at home were good ones. The worry I sometimes felt about Jaume was passing. I don't know if our daughters united or separated us: certainly it often seemed to me that we loved each other through them. When I took the cows to graze in the Solau meadows, the mad, wild joy of falling in love with Jaume, a paradise lost, would slowly knit back together in my memory, stitch by stitch. I couldn't imagine heaven as Monsignor Miquel described it. For me, it was just that strange force which changed my world.

Many times Elvira tore me from my thoughts and gave me a fright, something that made her break out laughing. She was growing up small but lively, with an energy that reminded me of Tia. She would come to take over from me so I could go and make dinner. Her teacher said she had a mind like quicksilver. I was delighted to think she would be able to look after herself better than I had in life.

One day in the meadow Elvira brought me some news. A letter had come from the cousins and Tia said she was thinking of going to Barcelona.

My heart jumped. Something terrible must have happened. Going so far away seemed such a dangerous thing to do. I went down the road as fast as my legs could carry me, as if I'd been told that the house was on fire. I'd left Elvira mid-sentence. I couldn't wait to find out what was going on. On the road I met Delina coming back with her cows. I was lucky to have her to distract me from my thoughts. Lively as ever, she told me that her older brother would soon be a priest, which made her very excited. He had told her that if she still hadn't agreed to marry someone by the time he had taken orders, she could keep house for him and take care of everything, from the holy vestments to the rectory. She would be well respected as the first lady of his parish. She knew that it would be a while before all this happened, but her life now had a direction, and she'd spent a long time without one. I still dared to say that in the meantime maybe some young man might want to marry her and she said No, God forbid. That she didn't see herself being any man's maid and that even the thought of it made her blood boil.

While I pondered what she meant by saying her blood would boil, I found myself threading through the first houses of the village and my former anxiety returned like a gust of wind. I bounded up the stairs three at a time and went to the kitchen. Tia was calmly peeling potatoes and Oncle was sitting by the fire with his pipe in his mouth. I knew then that nothing serious had happened and my first thought was that I wouldn't say anything of what Elvira had told me in case it annoyed Tia. But she spoke as soon as she saw me. Now, my girl, the Exposition is on in Barcelona and my cousin has asked me if I want to go. I think if I don't go to the capital now, I'll never go before I die, so if you can take care of the house and the children, I'm going to go two weeks from now. She added that the Exposition would be like a warehouse of all the best things that were made in lots of the countries of the world. Oncle said: And of course you have to give them your approval. He didn't say it in anger, but as if he felt envy that his wife was capable of being interested in something so unknown and far away...

All that meant nothing to him. Not that or even what happened in Montsent. Oncle liked the everyday and the routine more than anything else and Tia would often tell him off about it. If it were up to you, we'd all be living in just the one room in this house! She was exaggerating, of course.

Jaume wanted Elvira to go to the school in Mont-sent where they taught more reading, writing and arithmetic. He was anxious that she should learn as much as possible, and the great progress she had made the previous winter, as well as her teacher saying that she should go, decided it. The only thing holding her back was the hour and a half of walking she would have to do every day.

I told him that it might be good for her to learn to sew as well and he smiled. Of course! We thought it better to wait a little while and when Elvira reached the age of thirteen she could go into service in a nice house in Montsent and in the afternoon go to school for a few hours. That was what we said.

We'd gone out together, Jaume and I, to gather the animals from the side of Sant Damià mountain. It was a bright day and I felt as if I was looking at everything in a huge mirror. The wind was fresh, you could still make out the snow on the mountain tops, even though the new grass had come up some days before. The birches stretched their arms to the sky waiting for their soft foliage. We'd had to return early because I was looking after the house on my own. The girls stayed in the vegetable garden with Oncle while we went to bring the calves and cows back home.

We spent the time walking side by side and chatting. At night I would drop from exhaustion, but now I wanted to jump from one stone to the next to cross a stream or avoid a patch of nettles. The cows followed us, docile except when they found branches with new leaves on to eat. Then we had to tear them away and get them back on the road again. There was no need to worry about vipers, it was still too cold.

We went from speaking about the girls to things in general. Jaume said that he would have done anything to be able to go to Barcelona like Tia, that he was worried about the country's future, about justice. He said that we were abandoned on the mountain, that no one remembered the sons of the land who lived so far from where everything was decided.

When we talked about such matters the same thing always happened to me. A thick fog came over my brain and from there it passed to my heart. It left me frozen and in the dark. I was made to know what I saw, to speak about what I felt. I didn't know anything outside of Pallarès or Montsent or Ermita. I'd heard of Barcelona, of the sea, even of Madrid, of the King. It all seemed to me like one of the stories my father used to tell round the fire. I didn't believe all that really existed. I thought it was a trick, like Soledat Estevet having a claim to the throne of England. Perhaps that was why when I saw Jaume's eyes shining as he spoke of these strange things, the ground beneath me moved and I couldn't find true north. Instead of me guiding the animals, it felt like they were leading me. At moments like this, Jaume and I were as different as night and day, and that difference made me tremble more than when he left to go away for a whole week's work.

We arrived before it got dark. Thursday was ending and tomorrow was another day of work. That Sunday Tia would arrive with a face so radiant that I didn't recognize her. Words couldn't describe the Exposition and how well her relatives had treated her, especially Ventura, the daughter of her cousin Tomàs, who had walked everywhere with her.

She spoke of the pavilions, the gardens and so many things that couldn't compare to anything we knew in Pallarès. Only to the mountains and rivers, perhaps.

Oncle became ill in the autumn. It seemed to be because of all the hard work in the summer, but winter was approaching and he didn't get better. The doctor from Montsent said that if the burning sensations hadn't eased by Christmas, he would visit again and prescribe something for him. Squatting in a corner, Oncle payed no attention to anything. He hardly spoke and he didn't complain. He spent the odd while telling stories to the girls, but he did it when the grown-ups were busy far away from the kitchen. I never knew whether he liked doing this with the children or if he just wanted to help us. If he wasn't well enough to work, then at least he would entertain the children so that we could work.

By All Saints', Tia had begun putting an ointment made with snake oil and a blend of herbs on his stomach. I never found out where she'd got the recipe. Oncle let her do it but he didn't get better. He barely ate and wasn't sleeping at night.

We didn't need the doctor from Montsent to come again after all. On 8th December, the day of the Immaculate Conception, Oncle abandoned us in the ship that he had helped to sail.

I don't know if we always need to miss someone to know that we loved them, but that's how it happened to me. While he was alive I didn't have time to work out whether what I felt was love or a mixture of gratitude and concern. When he died, I felt pangs of love for this man who had for so long been a father to me. Maybe he hadn't done it with enthusiasm, which wasn't part of his character, but he had certainly shown good will. I promised myself I would make all my family happier and let them know I loved them and lived to make them happy. Above all poor Tia, who had become rather withdrawn despite her strong and active character.

As they say, sometimes sorrow marks a family for her own. Some months later, in March 1931, the news arrived that my mother had died. Jaume wanted to go with me to Ermita, but Tia wouldn't allow it. After all she was my mother's sister. We both hurried there.

I found my father and brothers and sisters in floods of tears. I couldn't accept that I hadn't been able to say goodbye to the woman who had brought me into the world. Just then I thought I understood my husband when he said we were so poor… and that it cost so much to go from one place to the other that when we arrived we were often too late.

Nothing and no one could console me. My father had aged a lot since Angeleta's baptism. My brothers and sisters were like distant relatives to me. I'd stopped being from there and I belonged elsewhere. At the same time, I couldn't help thinking about my life since I'd left my parents' house. The days seemed to have flown by, and I wondered if maybe my mother had never got over the pain of giving away a daughter. But that was the past and life went on. When we left Ermita, my eyes were numb from crying and my head heavy, and I thought, Who knows whether I'll ever come back, and that I'd lost the deepest of my roots there.

In Pallarès, the house, shrouded in mourning, had become quieter. The noise and uproar of my daughters seemed less jarring, perhaps because they were growing up or because I was thinking deeply and didn't hear it.

But a strange happiness was to enter our house very soon, announced by Jaume. King Alfonso XIII had left the country and the Republic had just been proclaimed. I didn't see this as any great happiness to speak of, but Jaume's joy flowed from his lips and hands and it was contagious. He grabbed me and took me out onto the street where people had gathered to talk. It was still cool but a sleepy spring sun was shining. I was blinded by so much light and overwhelmed by the sound of the word on everyone's lips – Republic.

A rumour went round that someone would come up from Montsent that evening to the school to explain what this change meant. The next day Tia told me that as she went into the school the Augusts were coming out, swearing and purple with rage. She was just in time to see Jaume jumping down from a table with the King's portrait in his hand. All that was left on the wall was a light patch and a nail.

In spring and autumn, when it has rained enough and the sun has warmed the earth, two types of mushrooms that are good to eat grow in rows in the meadows.

One sort is earth-coloured and delicate-looking, with a long straight stalk and a cap with dense gills underneath. The other is white and sprawling. It has a short thick stalk and the gills are a brownish colour. *Carreretes* and *moixarrons* are highly prized for eating raw, but both are also left to dry in sieves and are a precious resource in winter when there are none. Dried, they lose much of their smell and weight but just a handful gives an excellent flavour to rice or any rabbit, chicken or beef stew.

The meadows near the village yielded mushrooms, *carreretes* mostly, but not in great quantities. When we went to graze or divert the water from one part of the meadow to another, everyone would gather the ones they found in their meadows. But to have a year-round supply it was necessary to do a day trip.

That May of 1931 a fair-sized group of women from Pallarès gathered to pick *carreretes* and *moixarrons* on the mountain. On the way, we collected Jaume's sister-in-law, Agnès, and two or three other young women from Sarri came with us. Jaume had let them know we would be going that Wednesday. There were around ten or eleven of us.

I had met Delina beforehand and we brought two baskets each. Would we fill them? In the smallest we were carrying the food. Bread and ham. And we would find lots of water.

We left at daybreak and at the beginning we were as excited as little girls because we had finally enough time to talk to each other properly. When the going got steep, though, we held our tongues to save our breath.

I liked this outing. I was in the meadows, following the darker grass of the tracks thinking about nothing except finding a big patch of mushrooms and filling my basket. The walk was hard but, after going up so far, it was easy enough to walk down again. From where we were you could see all the villages as if they were close by, with the black slates of the roofs and the occasional plume of smoke revealing signs of life. We stopped at the top to eat, red-faced and with a light wind on our necks, before we started the painstaking search for mushrooms. Who would want to serve the stew of the *Festa Major* without *carreretes*? For those who really knew how to enjoy mushrooms the *moixarrons* were the great prize, and we would make omelettes with them raw.

Elvira had wanted to come with me, but I told her to stay and help at home. She was becoming a young woman now and only her wretched jealousy marred her sweetness. When Delina and I were talking about her, Delina told me something that shocked me. Before I'd had Angeleta, she'd heard how the women who chatted in the plaza – Mrs Sebastià, Mrs August, old lady Jou, the baker's wife and others – used to tell the children that if they didn't have siblings they should make the most of it because when one did come along, boy or girl, they wouldn't be laughing much. She'd heard comments like this many times. And much worse: that they wouldn't be loved any more, their mothers would only care about the baby, and that the best they could hope for was only having to share everything with their new brother or sister.

All this left me very upset and I felt for Elvira. If I'd known what they'd said, she would have come with me that day even though I felt such a long walk wasn't good for a young girl like her. I couldn't understand those people. Why did they do it?

Luckily we found mushrooms everywhere. If we hadn't, thinking about what Delina had told me might have made me really sick at heart. But there were mushrooms. It was as we'd hoped: it had rained, there had been sun and the earth was full and gave up its fruit. Tia would be happy. Seeing the *moixarrons* and *carreretes* poking their noses out of the grass – what a joy!

Summer was coming, bringing work that began unexpectedly but kept you breathlessly busy until the end of August. Then a few thunderstorms would sweep away the heat, and afterwards it would only be really hot for a moment or two at midday if there were no clouds covering the sun.

That year, 1932, the cousins didn't come up from Barcelona for the *Festa*, but I remember it as one of the nicest ever. Jaume didn't want us to miss a single dance. We were like sweethearts. I remember spinning with the music and the cool air on my burning cheeks. Flower dances, couples' dances... we did them all. After going to eat, we came back to dance until the early hours. I couldn't help remembering my first dance with Jaume. Was he thinking of it too? Just as on that day, I saw many people staring at us. Was it envy? He didn't notice. He just seemed to be living in the moment. In his arms I felt safe and secure, as if he would protect me from anything. That made me happy and scared me at the same time. I was struck by a terrifying thought: what would I be without him? But the accordion didn't stop and neither did I, as if I had wings on my feet.

Even today I can see Angeleta watching out of the corner of her eye as her father led me out to dance to the medley of tunes which signalled the end of the dancing in the afternoon. And halfway through, Elvira looking steadily at a boy who had brought her something to eat. At twelve she had the air of a bud about to burst into flower, with curly, silky chestnut hair that was still parted in two plaits, honey-coloured eyes, freckles around the nose and small, finely-drawn lips. Then I turn to look at Angeleta's small curly head as she dances with a slightly older girl, then again at Elvira, who waves and smiles. Before the last songs begin I tell Jaume that I am expecting and in the hustle and bustle I don't know if he has heard me. He carries on spinning me round, I can't see his eyes, only the down beside his ear. When the music stops, his smile makes me start breathing again. Will it be a boy this time?

Yes, I was hoping for a son. The girls were already young women and after the first year, bringing them up had flown by. They had been raised to respect Tia's authority – they called her grandmother. They had a father they adored but who was away a lot, and a mother they treated more like a big sister. I too was under Tia's daily orders, just like them, even when I didn't want to be. I thought of the last time I'd been upset and had to go through it alone, when my aunt and uncle had kept the milk from the girls because the calves needed it. I hadn't protested. I'd even not told Jaume about it, so there wouldn't be a fuss.

I wanted a boy. I don't know why. Maybe to protect us in the future, because he wouldn't do anything he didn't want to do, he wouldn't say he was fine when he was sick, and he wouldn't see pitch black as white.

Before dinner we went out to have a drink with a whole crowd of couples. The atmosphere was very animated. Aleix from Sarri came over and spoke to us about the water situation. Jaume said that Aleix could count on him, that he would go there the very next Monday. It was a matter of diverting it from a shaded area, where it flowed freely, to the meadows and houses in the sunny area of the village. The problem was that it would have to pass through a sliver of land belonging to the Alimbaus, the richest people in the village, and they didn't want to have anything to do with it. Jaume said it would have to go through the courts if there was no other way.

Fresh water going through the meadows from one side to another, flowing from the spring above.

Water filling the basins and the sink to do the washing.

After we'd finished the wine and *xolís* sausage we had ordered, we strolled home. It was starting to get cold, and we would need to bring overcoats if we were going out to dance again.

Jaume wasn't around much those days. He had been made a justice of the peace and he said that now was the time to bring water to Sarri de Dalt.

He had joined the Republican Left, which was the party of the *Generalitat* government. He had explained all this to me. It was a government in Barcelona which made deals with the one in Madrid. The president was from Lleida and was named Lluís Companys. He was a man who loved the workers and above all those who worked the land. Like us, he said. When I listened to him, it was easy to understand, but what he had joined was strange to me... and I must admit it worried me a little. What if Monsignor Miquel was right for once and Jaume got involved in wanting to fix what couldn't be changed... I didn't respond as he explained all this, and when he saw I was a bit sulky, he said, Don't worry, woman, I'm doing it all for good reasons. And then he suggested:

When we go to make hay this afternoon in Solau meadows we could go fishing in the river.

How quickly the shadows of the trout slipped under the rocks! Elvira was as smart as a fox, she'd learnt to fish by hand and very few got away from her. She didn't use tricks like swirling the water with a branch of mullein, which makes the trout drunk so they can be caught even by unskilled hands. That's not an honourable contest, Elvira would say, it gives no satisfaction at all. It's just cheating.

That evening they caught eight. That was enough. The dark grey scales with black and silver dots on its belly. Cooked on a hot stone with pieces of bacon, they were so good! Tia came along with salad, pickle, bread and wine.

While they finished haymaking, Angeleta accompanied me to find clover for the rabbits. When we were picking it, she found strawberries. Her little nose wrinkled as she concentrated on picking them. So tiny, red, fragrant, soft, easily squashed if you tugged them too forcefully... And Angeleta's little lively eyes, hers honey-coloured too, and her animated voice: Mama, I've found lots here!

The angels in the church at Pallarès didn't have eyes on their wings. I must admit that I didn't understand much when it came to religion and Monsignor Miquel's sermons often lost me. He would start with one thing then speak at great length before pausing. By the time he went onto something else, I'd already gone home, to the meadows, or even further, to the eyes of the angels of Ermita, which gazed at me unblinking so that I would tell them the truth about whether I had been good.

That Sunday, however, Monsignor Miquel's sermon touched on more earthly things, and when he began to speak about the men of this village, I held on to what he was saying as if I were holding the reins of a horse. He said that you couldn't shift things from where God had placed them, that every day man's desire to feel better than he was grew stronger, but that he did things without asking himself if he was going against the will of Our Lord, who had said, This way shalt thou run and no other way. When I heard him talking about running this way, I thought of the water for Sarri. But he couldn't possibly be referring to that. I continued to listen: there was an established order one had to accept, whether we were born rich or poor, sick or healthy. That in the eyes of God we were all equal before death. And that was what mattered. That all this recent talk of freedom and justice was driving people mad, including those doing the talking, who were also risking eternal damnation. In the first pew, right next to the pulpit, old lady Sebastià was nodding her head as if she agreed with everything. He finished by addressing the women and said we had to lead our men towards God and guide them when we saw they were lost. If we didn't, divine retribution would fall on the whole family.

When he finished preaching, Tia gave me a nudge and we exchanged meaningful glances. As we left, she told me that Monsignor Miquel had always been an arselicker when it came to the rich and now he was talking rubbish about things that had nothing to do with him. Tia didn't beat around the bush, and that was when I understood the sermon had been aimed at me. It made me want even more to forget everything that had been said as soon as possible. I had enough to do with just thinking about the amount of work there was to do at home and about my belly, which at the church door was the subject of conversation, friendly words and sideways glances.

The girls wanted a boy too and this brought them together. One was knitting a pair of socks and the other was sewing a little cotton shirt. I was exhausted, especially my legs, and the days felt very long despite the fact that Elvira was helping eagerly. If it was a boy, Jaume had already found him a name. He would be called Mateu, like Jaume's father. If it was a girl, he wanted her to be named after me. Sometimes I heard the name Mateu and liked it. Sometimes the sound of it made me think of matadors and death. But I often found myself with the name on my lips and I got used to it. And if a boy didn't want to be born? That bird of ill omen, Soledat, hadn't said anything to me, which gave me hope.

I'd been dreaming. I was dancing and when the music stopped I looked at my partner and he had no face. I was sure I was dancing with Jaume, but his features were erased... The plaza was full, but all the people I saw there were strangers to me. I only recognized Martí Sebastià on top of the stone platform playing music. He was laughing like a madman, with plenty of sweat trickling down his face, and showing all his teeth. I wanted to run but my legs wouldn't move. Then I felt the tiny hand of little Mateu in mine, pulling me until I found myself at the steps of home, all alone.

I sat up in bed wanting to shout out loud. Jaume had already got up and it was just becoming light. It was the day he had to go to Sarri.

In the dream, Mateu was a bit bigger. He must have been six years old, and when I had that dream he was only three. His hand in the dream, though, was very small. I could almost still feel it

Suddenly we see Delina coming towards us, flapping her arms like a bird. Mateu laughs at her. She arrives, hot, as red as a tomato. She speaks. I came to tell you that at the market I met old man Sastre from Torve. He asked me to tell you that they have settled on your Elvira for their son. And she adds, They're a very good family, don't think about it too long.

I am astonished. But she's not even sixteen yet... and here's Delina advising me, Delina who didn't want to get married and will soon end up being a housekeeper for her brother.

I listen as she continues. If it sounds good to you, you could meet at the market next Monday to arrange for them to visit each other. Try to convince your husband. Now I must hurry, we have a cow that wants to calve...

She's gone before I have a chance to speak and leaves me feeling as if I'd been run over. I watch her racing towards her house. I think of Elvira. Maybe time is passing too quickly. Just then what I dreamt comes back to me and I feel a chill down my spine.

Barcelona, 20th July 1936

Mrs Encarnación Martí

Dearest cousin and all the family,

I hope that on receiving these lines you find yourself enjoying good health as we are here, thanks be to God.

We just received your letter concerning our arrival up there. We have decided that, for the moment, we are going to say that we are not coming. The news about the uprising is rather worrying, and we think that because of the insecurity it would be better to wait until things have calmed down before we go away anywhere.

Please do not think that it was an easy decision to make; Ventureta was really looking forward to it and she does nothing but cry and say she wants to go up north. Thanks be to God she is much better, so it was not necessary that we came for her health; but please believe that we are all sorry and will truly miss this longed-for holiday and the days out and the fine food up there. We are sorry that dear Conxa has already made up the rooms, but we must resign ourselves. It must be God's will.

We are sending you some fabric we had bought to make a dress for the girls. Well, I say girls, but Elvira must be a woman now, and Ángela too.

We hope for everyone's sake that nothing will happen and that we might still come up in August.

There is nothing else to say save that everyone here sends everyone there much love, especially from Ventureta and my wife Elisa.

Your devoted cousin,
TOMÁS OLIVELLA

After the news that some soldiers had revolted in Africa, everything turned upside down at home. Our cousins didn't come up. Tia was in bed with a stomach bug that left her exhausted. Between work outside the village and the trips to Sarri, where they had just installed the water, Jaume was never at home. Monsignor Miquel complained, as much in the pulpit as on the street, that so much disorder would necessarily have to be met with order and that this Republic was a disaster. The sermon lasted longer than the Mass. Clearly he wanted to vent his feelings, because the sermons had nothing to do with the gospel of the day. What's more, I continued to have that awful dream almost every night. The children were the only ones who were the same as ever. Elvira, happily in service at Montsent. She was learning so much, so happy to be there. In sewing class they showed her how to make a dress... Mateu, thin as always, but strong as a rock. Angeleta, helping me in everything and everywhere, poor little thing.

Little by little news comes. Some people talk about fighting and deaths in the south of Spain… others talk about atrocities in Barcelona. They say that the priests have gone into hiding. Ours hasn't been seen for two days. Jaume is exultant. He keeps saying that what the people have decided freely cannot easily be set aside, not even with guns. What does he mean, the people? The people means all the men and women who live in this country. I back away from these conversations and feel suffocated. Better not to ask anything. Today he told me off because I mentioned the marriage proposal for Elvira. As if it's my fault someone wants to marry her. Don't I say and keep saying that she is still a little girl? But he was like a wild animal. Is it that she's a nuisance? A nuisance, my daughter? And then he went on about the heir's family. He shouted: What do they want with a little girl of sixteen? Has the world gone mad?

Big tears roll down my cheeks. My heart sinks. I say I am going to wash clothes in the river and leave the room. Jaume has stopped talking. I leave him staring at the glass in the window.

Part Three

The rattling of the engine made me drowsy, but I was wide awake. I wasn't dreaming now. On one side Elvira, on the other Angeleta and faces all around me. All unfamiliar, all quiet and withdrawn. No, this was no dream. It was real.

They'd called at midday and asked in Spanish for the wife and children of *Jaime* Camps. Tia had answered all their questions calmly. I'd just obeyed. I had to get into the lorry with my children. We could snatch a little to eat for the day. Quickly. At the last minute, Tia had given a mattress to Elvira. It seemed unnecessary to me, but I didn't say anything. I looked at the weapons and those tall strong boys, and they looked at Elvira out of the corners of their eyes. I just went along. Old Mrs Jou came and asked them to have mercy and let the little boy stay with his grandmother because he's only six and he's sick. They pushed her away but they didn't take the boy, who clutched Tia's black dress like a leaf curled up by the wind against an old tree trunk.

And no news from him, from Jaume. They came for him at daybreak. I was still in bed and so were the girls and little Mateu. I think they didn't hear anything. Three short sharp knocks on the door. In Spanish: *Camps, Jaime...* – then all of his names – *Justice of the Peace of the town of Pallarès under the Republic... come with us.* As I got dressed quickly, I thought the baker had been right the night before. Get out of here Jaume, take my word for it. I've heard they want everyone who's stood out in some way. They're out for revenge because the guard at the Algorri bridge was killed. And Jaume said, I haven't done anything wrong and I don't have to hide from anything.

And then... before he'd even combed his hair, a hug. A goodbye. I didn't cry, but inside I felt as if they had wrenched my soul from my body. And he just says: Don't worry... don't do anything. And seeing him from behind, walking between the guards. He looked much smaller than usual to me. The village seemed deserted. There was nobody on the street. Roseta Sebastià poked her head out onto the balcony. She wasn't afraid. She gave a twisted little smile as they passed underneath her. The priest's housekeeper also opened her balcony door but she looked out cautiously, without allowing herself to be seen. I had no doubt: there were eyes watching behind every window.

Now, in the lorry, Mundeta from Sarri comes up to me and I begin to recognize other faces. She tells me they are taking us to Montsent, what will become of us? In the morning they'd come looking for her son too. She's a big woman, Mundeta. She has white hair and very tired eyes. There are people from Torve, from Sant Damià, from lots of villages in the region. One woman remembers me from Ermita and tells me that my father is very old, but he and my brothers and sisters are well. I hear it all like you hear rain from inside a cave, that doesn't make you wet or even splash you. I am pleased to hear it but feel no happiness.

They take us to Montsent prison. I didn't even know where it was. The worst is not knowing anything. Elvira moves around and talks to everyone, even the jailers. Most of them are almost as young as she is. She does what I am not capable of doing. I feel like a stone after a landslide. If someone or something stirs it, I'll come tumbling down with the others. If nothing comes near, I'll be here, still, for days and days...

Angeleta doesn't move either, clinging to my skirts. All of us are women and children. At least fifteen. What we have in common is that someone close to us has been taken. For a while no one says anything. Then, timidly, someone begins to talk.

Our side of the river had already been taken by the nationalists, the Blackshirts. The other side was still in the hands of the Reds. There were families who wanted to cross to the Red side, which you did by the Algorri bridge. After the guard there was killed last night, the way over was clear. They say that they spoke to all the rich families in the valley. A priest gave some names too. That's how they knew who to take.

Now I feel like I'm out in the open under a light rain that gradually soaks me through to my spine. I shake violently, silently torn to pieces. My God, are we so bad that we deserve to suffer so much?

At dusk they give us each a spoonful of soup in a bowl, without even a drop of oil. My throat's so dry it's like swallowing thorns. Angeleta has started to move around a bit. She is playing with a younger girl. Elvira says something to me from time to time. Her serenity calms me. I think, she says, we're going to spend the night here.

Will it rain? Beyond the grille above our heads, we can see a scrap of sky. How slowly time passes when you have to wait but you don't know what you're waiting for!

I see Elvira discussing something with the soldiers at the door. Now they are taking her out. Oh God! What's going on? People look at me. I can't tell whether they resent me or pity me. She comes back. She is carrying two blankets. She comes over to me. She has spoken with Tia. Mateu is with Delina, he's fine. Tia also said that she's gone to protest to Elvira's employers, and at the rectory, and wherever she thought people could do something, but with no results yet. How brave of her, poor woman...

It's already past midday and they haven't given us anything to eat. Does that mean they're letting us go?

I am more resigned. We have to get through this, and who knows, perhaps we'll all be back together again soon, discussing all this anguish as if it were water under the bridge.

We are in the lorry again. I think it's the same one as yesterday. Elvira chats to the soldiers... They joke. We are going downhill, towards the plain. Everything looks so pretty. It doesn't seem possible that anyone should have to suffer, however poor and insignificant. The birds are singing all around, the river murmurs on our left, the sun has finally come out from behind the clouds and it's hot. The pines above, the ashes and the poplars nearby are still. Only we are moving, always downwards. We see no one on the roads or in the villages we pass through, only groups of armed soldiers like those guarding us. We don't know where we're going. We are silent. We still have a little bit of food. We share it with the people next to us. Here there are no differences. We are all one family, such an unhappy family. I pick the crumbs from my skirt, one by one. It's difficult, everything is moving. I'm not hungry but who knows when I will taste homemade bread again?

We have been stopped here for a while. I don't know what they are discussing among themselves. Elvira comes over and whispers in my ear that for the time being we are going to Noguera. We will certainly spend the night there. I look at her and she seems as pretty as an angel to me. Even with her hair unwashed and uncombed. Of the three, she looks the most like her father... And him? How is he? Poor man. He'll be thinking about us a lot.

I'd never been to Noguera. It's big. The capital of the region. Here we see plenty of people. They look at us from a distance as if we've got the plague. And we have: fear, uncertainty, suffering... Now they say the prison is full. We have to stay in a warehouse above a garage until tomorrow. Luckily, it's big. We stay close together instinctively, to support each other. We go to unroll the mattress to rest our heads. But what's happening? Elvira clutches my neck and squeezes me so tightly that she almost chokes me. She's crying, she cries without stopping... I can't make her answer. What's wrong? What's wrong, girl? When I begin to tell her in a low voice, Look, all this will pass, maybe tomorrow... she hushes me. Mother, Mother, this morning they killed them all, near the bridge. A soldier I know from Montsent told me, just now... The news spreads through the room. The sound of wailing and crying is broken by names being called out and by periods of silence, by people falling to the ground and by the terror of the children, who don't know what to do. I feel an axe-blow to the centre of my heart, but not one tear nor cry nor drop of blood comes out of me. I embrace my two daughters, an arm around each and I feel their tears like a stream that cannot wash my wound. Angeleta buries her head in my skirt and I caress her hair with my right hand. I coil a lock around my fingers and I think of Jaume's face, always smiling. A young woman cries and pulls at her hair. She rolls around on the floor making choking noises. And now at last I notice how my cheeks are slowly getting wet. Instead of a cry escaping, I feel a very strong pain in my throat, as if I am being strangled...

A soldier comes in, his eyes bulging out of his head. He shouts in Spanish, *Silencio y a dormir.* Shut up and go to sleep.

I'd always been afraid of death. Of death at home. Of having to speak in whispers and look at someone who'll be carried off feet-first the next day to be buried in a hole. Of being kissed by everyone, of false condolences and sincere condolences and of seeing the reddened eyes of people I love. And now I didn't even have a dead body. I was more afraid and more anguished not to have seen his body still, not to have seen his beautiful cheeks, once the colour of pomegranate flowers, pale and waxen. I was sad and I had no body with eyes to close, to sit up with or buy a coffin for or accompany to the grave with freshly-picked flowers and weep over gently. He'd gone as quickly as a rose cut from the bush and I'd no last memory of him except a little spark as he looked at me during our strange goodbye. I knew he was dead and I would never again have him at my side, because war is an evil that drags itself over the earth and leaves it sown with vipers and fire and knives with points upright. And I was barefoot with my children, and I had nothing apart from still being alive. I didn't even have a mourning dress because his death wasn't like others, it was a murder that had to be forgotten immediately. His name was to be entombed behind eyelids and mouths with thick cement. I knew he was one of the ones they'd killed because they were taking me in the lorry of sorrow to Aragón. Because they had to take us wretches away from the only thing left to us: our misery, with our scrap of sky and our vale of tears.

When I realized that we were alone, like a flock without a shepherd, perhaps with the wolf circling, a great sense of abandonment came over me. It broke my heart that I didn't feel I had the strength to be a mother. I was stunned behind a wall of sadness and since I couldn't scream or lose control, I wanted to stay still, unmoving, unthinking. Focused on sorrow and without hope. The girls had to keep on living and I wanted to die. I felt that if I just stayed still with that hell inside, I was bound to explode and then it would be goodbye Conxa. But abandoning the girls to their fate tormented me and when Elvira told me to eat, after I'd refused any food for two days, I did as she said. I had to force the bread down my throat, which wasn't allowing anything to pass, like a reed stalk that hasn't been cleaned through properly… all under the watchful eye of my eldest daughter, roles reversed for the first time. I wanted so much to shout, Enough!

Elvira adapted to her new life. The young can do anything. Even though she was knocked back many times. Because she moved around, spoke to everyone, wasn't ashamed of anything. They called us Reds. They'd also killed men from where we were staying. Many others had gone to France. Even entire families, people said.

The camp we stayed in was beside a village a little smaller than Montsent. One day a girl of about the same age insulted Elvira because she said the Reds had killed her boyfriend. Luckily, Elvira was accompanied by a boy from Aragón who defended her, poor boy. There were those who wanted us not only to suffer but to feel guilty as well. Why do hundreds of stones always fall at once?

Six people were sleeping crossways on our mattress. There were lice and, as much as we tried to wash ourselves conscientiously, we couldn't avoid them completely. We ate badly but they didn't starve us. We worked: cleaning, in the infirmary, sewing... It was full of Italians. They scared us, we stayed away from them as much as we could.

The days weighed on my heart like flagstones. The endless tears had dried, everything seemed like a nightmare that had to end, one day or another. Beyond the nightmare, I thought I could make out hope. The hope of going home. Maybe they'd lied. It couldn't be true that they killed him, so full of life, without any proof. They couldn't just have said: You, you and you... Maybe they were in prison or evacuated like us. What could a soldier know? I didn't share any of these thoughts with the girls. I kept them to myself like a secret that, soon, when they became reality, would fill the girls with joy. Silence calmed me and gave me strength. Keeping quiet, daydreaming about the way the hours of a day turn out. Any old day, a normal day or a bad day. Of the day when a bolt of lightning killed a cow and you were annoyed by it, and the day that everything seemed to fall into place. The hay in the haystack, the chickens roosting, the cows quiet in the stable, and everyone having dinner at the table. No, I didn't say anything to the girls. They needed to move on. What had happened was a huge blow to them but there was no point in thinking about it. You have to keep going. They couldn't fall back on hoping that it wasn't true... I, on the other hand, I needed to go back just to be able to breathe a little.

They didn't tell us anything. How long would they keep us here? What were we doing there? What were women and children good for up there? We barely understood the orders they gave us...

The land there seemed good. There wasn't plenty of water like we had, true. It was lower and warmer. The people must have lived well, before, but then they didn't have a normal life either. Only soldiers here and there, orders, shouting and silence.

They made us pray in the morning and at night. I didn't know the prayers in Spanish and I just pretended by moving my lips. I didn't want to learn to pray again. Inside I was already praying to God and I spoke to Him for a long time. I explained things to Him and I begged Him. But always on the inside. Like two friends who know each other and can tell each other everything just through their eyes. No need to open your mouth, just find a bit of the pain and pull at it gently like wool from a skein, let it unravel, unravel... until you can't see colours any more because your eyes have flooded but it's not tears that fall from your eyes. The wool you were unravelling has turned into a sheet of water slipping down your cheek, and just as you were going to let out a sob, you realize you're not alone. A knot forms in your throat, causing such a strong pain but you swallow and swallow, until slowly you untangle the knot and you're left with the skein. A fragment of sorrow, knot and all, has gone down directly to your stomach.

When they entered Barcelona, someone must have said that they could send us home. It had been five and a half weeks. When we got to the chapel at Sant Josep, which meant we were within sight of Pallarès, my legs were still trembling.

Before we left Montsent, they'd sent us to see a lieutenant colonel in his study, four at a time. The three of us went in with Mundeta, who'd become like family by now. He kept us standing by the desk for a while, with a soldier guarding the closed door. He made us give our names and after that he did all the talking, in Spanish. "*Our country's shame is over. Thanks be to God we are saved. We expect your conduct to be impeccable from now on. If you are good Spaniards, then you will have nothing to fear. Now go, and don't forget what I said.*" He had a thick black moustache that didn't suit his very small nose. I don't remember his eyes. I'd only given him a quick glance as we went in. The whole

102

time he was speaking, I looked at my skirts, which had a pleat that was fraying more with each passing day, and my toes, poking out of my espadrilles. They tried to make us feel guilty. It was the same old song over and over, and I was afraid for my daughters. We all behaved as if we were mute, and when Mundeta seemed about to open her mouth, I squeezed her hand and luckily the soldier at the door was already opening it for us.

Home on foot, from Montsent, we looked at everything as if for the first time. Clematis was blooming, budding everywhere. It grew among the brambles, fearless of the thorns. White clematis. Clematis, tender but strong. Clematis to tie the sheaves. Clematis to make skipping ropes for the children. I plucked a soapwort bud just coming into flower and the sweetness of its scent made me so happy that I cried. Then in the middle of the road all three of us hugged each other and couldn't stop crying, our tears starting each other off. I thought I heard something and said: That's enough, maybe people have heard that we're back. I felt my cheeks burn as we walked past the first houses. Like the day we left, there was nobody to be seen.

Night was falling. Time to shut the cows into the yard. Time to make dinner. Time to dawdle a moment at the fountain to discuss something, but only as long as it takes to say a quick Lord's Prayer!

From beside the trough I saw a woman appear. It was Delina, who ran and threw herself into my arms. She kept saying: How awful, Conxa... It was then I understood I wasn't dreaming and that it was real. Gently, I let go of Delina and walked towards home, my feet heavy. As soon as we came through the door little Mateu grasped my legs and the girls fell into Tia's arms. It was the second time I'd seen her cry...

And then dragging the mattress up the stairs and sitting on the bench with my little boy in my lap and letting Elvira and Angeleta explain everything, jumbled-up, and Tia asking question after question but giving nothing away herself.

And accepting that Jaume was no longer Jaume. He had gone like a gust of wind, and I didn't have the heart to breathe or to do anything or be like before. I had one hand on the table he had made, and I yearned for the wood to tear me apart so completely that there wouldn't be a scrap of me left.

What surprised me most when I went around the house were the cobwebs everywhere. I saw that Tia had become really old. I went into the kitchen and there was shadowy fluff in the corner of the ceiling, like a spy. Going into our bedroom, I mean my bedroom now, and approaching the pillow, small arms resisted mine. Long cobwebs stood guard around the bed...

When I got to the threshold, I would think about the two of you not being there. I would start shaking in sorrow and anger. I haven't been able to set foot inside, Tia confessed.

I began to remove the cobwebs with a broom. Sometimes the spiders would escape their lodging in a surprised flurry. I would immediately press down once or twice with the broom as hard as I could until nothing was moving underneath, as if the spider was one of my nightmares. I started thinking again that maybe it wasn't true that Jaume was dead, and now I was back home suddenly I'd hear his voice on the stairs saying, What's for dinner in this house today?

But when I'd killed several and I was cleaning the broom on the back wall of the haycock, where the stones stuck out and you could remove all the dust, hot tears started to flow without warning, and I tried to stop them even though I was all alone. Because I was sure I would never again hear the voice which had said the nicest things that had ever been said to me. I was thirty-seven and I was sure of it. Then Mateu appeared with a baby rabbit in his arms. He said it was his and we were never to kill it and eat it. I dropped the broom, and hugged him so hard that he became frightened, because I was sobbing more and more desperately. As I grabbed him the rabbit jumped out of his arms and my little boy ran after it and away from me as fast as his legs could carry him.

It was a spring clean I'll never forget. I didn't want to leave a corner untouched, as if I was afraid the lice from the camp might have jumped onto the walls. I didn't want to be spied on as we slept at night, no matter how small the eyes were.

I got angry with the girls because they only wanted to freshen the house up, and I screamed at them that we needed more than just a once-over after what we'd been through. They looked at me with their eyes wide with surprise that I saw turn to compassion. And they ended up saying yes to everything just at the point where I had given up and was about to say that it didn't matter.

I gave myself the same treatment and scrubbed vigorously from head to toe as if my body was filthy with blood and fear and misery and I could get it all off in the bath. I don't think I understood at the time that the problem wasn't in my skin or hair or nails... And when I saw myself, my slim body with its small breasts and striking nipples, I realized that I would never feel joy or pleasure in it again. I thought, people are very little but sometimes we think we really are something.

After the great purge and all the uproar, Tia didn't let me do anything else and I didn't want to either. I was relieved. I knew I was another Conxa, as if I'd lived many years in a month and a half.

Whenever someone talked about the war and I was there, people always expected me to have something to say but I never gave them the satisfaction. If everyone fell silent, however, I felt very uncomfortable and sometimes I noticed that my cheeks began to burn. If Soledat was there, she couldn't stop herself from getting people to ask me what happened to us in the war.

Why did people dedicate themselves to hurting us? Within a few days of our return from the camp they came filing through the house with the excuse that they were worried about us, today one, tomorrow another, and each one said he knew who was responsible for Jaume's death. They would accuse someone from our very town, sometimes a neighbour, and leave feeling so self-satisfied. My heart was broken and I didn't dare say that I didn't want to know. I put up with those denunciations with a great deal of patience, which I found by imagining that the person in front of me was there in good faith.

It was different when they came to find out how we were and see if we were selling the biggest meadows, which were the best, or maybe if we were thinking of getting rid of some cows... And you would say no, humbly, so you wouldn't have to hear people say to your face, You deserved what happened to you! There came a time when we didn't know if we were dealing with being unlucky or with being guilty of something. People seemed to expect us to behave as if we'd been defeated and show that we'd learnt our lesson, that we were inferiors who would beg like complete paupers to be treated normally by other people.

Elvira was made to cry many times. As she was the eldest, she had to put up with more. One day she was asked along with some other girls to help out in the Augusts' kitchen. They had a radio and the national anthem was played. Old Mrs August jumped up and stuck her arm out. The girls did the same. When it finished, she said to our girl in front of everyone: Elvira, your salute wasn't very enthusiastic, what's the matter? She never wanted to go back there again.

Delina was the only one who came to us out of pure compassion. She hadn't wanted to tell us anything. She came when she could and if I was darning, she helped me darn. If I was kneading, we kneaded and sometimes we spent the whole time without saying a word. I enjoyed her company precisely because of this. She knew as much as the others, but she never made an accusation against any person in particular. Only sometimes she would just say, There are bad people, Conxa, who don't forgive.

There was a lot of work and little food. Together, painfully and with big effort, we all kept the house running. Tia was responsible for the house and Elvira took charge of the land, which I would never have thought I could do. But we all put our backs into it and did what we could.

The days joined one to another in a long rosary without mysteries. Some passed quickly, others slowly. When you counted it up, a lot of time had gone by.

The days passed. Elvira was unmoved by the boys who courted her. It was hard to break the ice in the village, but slowly and sometimes secretly, proposals began to arrive. It was because they had seen her work. She did it like a man, whether it was mowing the grass or raking it, and if necessary, standing her ground like a man too.

One evening after dinner she said that she wished to marry outside Pallarès and renounce her rights to earn a living from the land. Tia predicted it would all end in tears. She would be hungry, since a man who lives only on a wage is lost, and soon enough we would see her walking up to the house clutching her belly in pain… Elvira let her speak, her face composed. I didn't dare to ruin her plans but I didn't know how to contradict Tia. I stayed quiet and reproached myself inwardly for it, because I think Elvira expected me to defend her. But when Angeleta began to tease her about the marriage, she went wild. Mateu was already nine years old. He was starting to help out around the house and he didn't dare say a word because he wasn't going to bite the hand that fed him. His big sister washed him, parted his hair, and shouted at him when he got dirty. Who would start a fight in his position?

When I went to take the animals to pasture, I would think about all these things. It was the task I liked best. I spent many hours alone with the animals and had time to lose myself thinking about the past and the present. The waving of poplar leaves took me away to my time in Ermita or the first days in my aunt and uncle's house. I was enchanted by the sparrows and when I had to shout at Fosca or Clapada to guide them back onto the track, my mind was blank. These were the best parts of my day. When I returned with the animals flicking their tails against the flies, I felt comforted.

The day after Elvira told us that she was going to marry a boy who worked in forestry and go to live in Noguera, I thought, walking home, that they didn't need me any more. It was a new idea, like a ray of sunlight filtering through the branches and blinding me.

Elvira hadn't married yet but she would. And she'd do well. Angeleta would marry as well. She was quiet, hard-working and sweet. None of that would go unnoticed. Besides, she was pretty.

And Mateu had Tia to show him what to do. She would be a mother to him. And at fifteen he would be a young heir. The moment the thought crossed my mind, I felt as if I'd been stabbed. Despite the pain, I repeated to myself: They don't need me any more.

And I didn't think of it again until the first night of the *Festa Major*. I heard the music of the party from my bed, faintly. Like a bird hearing a mating cry, I got up, put on my black dress and slowly, but deliberately, I went to the loft. Under the roof in a corner lay the wooden cradle where my three children had slept when they were small, and which their father had made with his own hands. It was simple, with just a zigzag pattern along the sides. I saw his tools in the open cupboard as well. But I didn't stop there. I opened the window and put my head out. The noise of the river filled me completely, along with the smell of green and tender foliage. It was far down but I could hear it very clearly and it seemed much more welcoming than the hell of my bed. I dragged the cradle a little way and stood it on its end under the window. As I raised my right foot to get up on it, I heard a soft sound nearby. Tia was looking at me wide-eyed. She said to me: Is it that you can't bear the noise, child? She put her right arm on my shoulder and like that, close to her body, small yet steady, I went down to my bedroom without a word.

My eldest daughter had been lucky. She already had a beautiful healthy son and instead of coming to beg food, we had to ask her to come up to help us in the summer. Angeleta couldn't do it because she had married into farming people and had enough work at home. Only the heir needed to marry and even though he was young, Tia and I began to lose patience because he didn't seem to put any effort into it. He was hard-working and skilful like his father. He'd grown up with a docile character, not the type to shout, still less give orders. He was kind-hearted and happy. He wasn't bad to look at. Tall, a little too thin perhaps, he had curly chestnut hair and large peaceful eyes, a long nose and a delicate mouth.

But the time had come that young women thought long and hard before settling in a farming household. I asked the girls to see if they could find him someone in Noguera or in Torrent. I thought: You will lose him. But he needed a wife and to keep the house running with children. What was he going to do with two old women?

While all this was bubbling in my head, Tia died. One morning, surprised that she hadn't already risen, I found her in bed like a shrunken sparrow. She went without giving us the least work. We didn't even have to make her a tisane. Had it not been for Mateu, her death would have left me completely forsaken. Her small wrinkled face, toothless in recent years, and more than anything her voice had been my sweetest companions on many long nights. To remember her, as if I saw her from a distance, I had the photograph my son-in-law from Noguera took of her in secret, because she didn't want her picture taken. Sitting in the meadow, with the cart full of grass opposite, she was turning to little Ramon who was listening to her nearby. She is wearing a black scarf low on her forehead and her face can't be seen clearly.

Now that I was alone, the idea of getting Mateu married began to worry me. If something happened to me, my son would have to leave everything to take care of me. And who would look after him?

I felt no peace until the day he went to Torrent to stay with his sister and go calling on a potential bride. A girl there had been recommended to us. She was the youngest of four, boys and girls. All were married apart from her and the second son. Neither poor nor rich, they earned their living from animals, milking and hunting. The father was a chamois hunter. She was said to be well-versed in running a house and working the land, and she knew how to sew and do arithmetic.

I thought a lot that day, alone at home. Soon it would be milking time. Sitting beside the window I heard Clapada grumbling in the stable. But there was still light and I wanted to finish patching that sheet. A young woman would come into this house where she didn't know a single room and become the mistress of it. I would give her the keys to all the doors so that those walls which had heard so many voices would shake with joy once again. Songs, children crying, the clatter of plates: all the rough and tumble of life that could bring colour to the shadows.

And this happy thought left me filled, inside, with sweet tears which I didn't want to explain to myself. I couldn't see what I was sewing. It had become dark. I had to go milk and little else. Not lay the table nor prepare the meal for the next day.

Remembering it now, I believe that night foretold the beginning of a new era of my life.

The day of the wedding I suffered a lot. We celebrated in Torrent. The girls were there, my two sons-in-law and the three grandchildren – Elvira's Ramon and Rita and Angeleta's Agustí. I was with people all day but I couldn't keep my thoughts from escaping to Pallarès, to Jaume's and my wedding day. I wanted to stop remembering but that only made my eyes fill with tears as if I was at a funeral. Perhaps that was why my daughter-in-law kept her distance from me, very shy, as if she was afraid to open her mouth to me.

Everything went well. A good dinner, jokes and laughter, and me trying to keep my feet on the ground. I couldn't believe that these two women with little children and the man marrying that day were my own children. How time had flown! I had to be a middle-aged or even an old woman. I'd never thought about it until that moment. The years after the war were a fixed point, immobile, all the same. I had stopped moving the morning the soldiers had knocked on the door. Maybe I'd lost myself in the camp at Aragon. That's why it now seemed strange to me that my children had grown up and I'd become old. A slow old woman who didn't make a sound, carried her weight but who thought of herself as a bit of a halfwit. And who all of a sudden realized that at last death was on its way because she was over fifty and she didn't want anything now or in the future.

But it's not we who decide how long we live. We can't say, I've had enough, I'm off now, or I'm happy now, I want to live longer. Of course I knew that, but I didn't understand it yet.

It makes me laugh to think that now. It's been my fate to live another thirty years and, although useless, I am still breathing.

The music hadn't ended – no, there was another song still to come. Some good things: knowing that the grandchildren were growing, seeing them once a year, attending the birth of the others, thinking we needn't lack anything if we worked, letting time numb bad memories... And on the other hand, the deepest silence. Learning that there is a type of person, people brought up strictly, who don't know how to respect people who don't order them around. I had to watch Mateu change, from quiet and happy to restless and surly. Marrying for convenience can turn out like that. You can get everything right except character. What happens when the potential bride and groom visit each other? Some time is spent in the dining room and dowries are discussed, the best sausage and a *porró* of wine are brought out. Then left alone, the couple say a few things to each other full of timidity and awkwardness.

It's a purchase like any other, but things that can't be measured come into it. A person is too much to be bought and too little to live as he pleases...

I contributed more than anyone to my son getting married and they say every sin has its penance. I certainly had mine.

It's true things weren't easy for them. Lluïsa did not really recover from the birth of their first child in the clinic at Noguera, and from then on she complained constantly. Mateu, who had hardly travelled in thirty years, was doing so every other minute. First to Noguera, again and again. To see what the doctors would say. Afterwards they headed to Lleida and later to Barcelona.

Appointments, travel and medicines that cost a lot of money. Whole days that the fields were abandoned even when the work couldn't wait for a day. Hurry, annoyance... I did what I could. I looked after the baby, the animals, the vegetable garden, the poultry, but I couldn't manage the work outside.

I remember that time of waiting. I knew that something was going to change. Because that dream of mine had not come true. The house was fuller, but not much happier. A sadness that

I'd never known had entered it. The sadness of those who find themselves unwell. Apart from the children's illnesses, or a cold or a bad back, the sicknesses we'd suffered hadn't lasted long. True, Oncle had been ill, but he was long-suffering and with an old man's conviction that his time to leave this world had come and that he didn't really want to get better.

Little Jaume would have taken all my time if I'd known how to arrange it, but his mother kept me away from him with the zeal for bringing up her child that a mother feels for her first-born. Lluïsa and I hadn't become close and even though I tried to do things as she liked, I never managed it. I think that every time she had to go to the doctor and leave the baby in my care was torture for her. I understood her but I didn't dare say anything to her because she was very nervous and moody. As if everyone else was to blame that she didn't feel well.

I watched the rain with little Jaume, and he turned his big black eyes on me when I started some story or other. The little drops chased each other over the glass and he didn't tire of listening patiently. But at dinnertime, it was the same as usual. He tried a few spoonfuls and there was no way he would swallow any more. I thought that the tension in the house took away his appetite, but I would have bitten my tongue off before saying it.

I think of that rainy afternoon as the closest memory of being with my grandson. As Jaume got older, and his brother Lluís after him, they would live far away from their grandmother, even though they might eat at the same table.

And I accepted it. Perhaps I had turned into a living stone, or it was just that I had never known how to rebel. To say, I am not dead yet or, Here, money is only used for this or that, and other things too. I felt that I was going to need to be strong, but I had no idea why.

One evening, everything outside was covered in snow and it was very cold. Mateu came to see me. He was so sweet, like he'd been before, that I didn't recognize him. Mother, we've looked at a porter's lodge in Barcelona. We get a salary and they give us a little flat between the ground floor and basement. We'll be close to the doctors there and we won't have to worry about the land...

Even if I had dared say, Leave me to stay here, I want to die on this land, it wouldn't have made any difference. I would have been told that I was mad, and what would I want to do alone in a big house? It would have made even less difference if I'd gone on to say that this was my house and that I'd spent my life on this land...

I didn't say anything, as if I thought it a good idea, as if the news came as no surprise.

I realized it wasn't true that I was resigned and didn't want to live. Now we were leaving, life meant staying close to where I'd been told Jaume was buried, pottering about, getting by without much enthusiasm, letting people say what they liked, keeping up what had cost us so much to get. So much effort, so much saving, so much misfortune. Now we were closing the door and going down the mountain, much further down than Noguera, more than twice as far down.

A house of seven floors, he had said, and I imagined it to be sky high.

I didn't want to be separated from my son, not at all, but I couldn't believe his promises that we'd come back when things got better. I remembered what Tia had said to me perhaps ten years before she died. The girls were still at home. I don't know what we were discussing, but she'd said that we wouldn't die there in that house, that life was too hard in those villages and that the young people growing up then wouldn't want to put up with it. I remember that as usual I didn't contradict her, but I thought she was exaggerating. I thought to myself that this was old age speaking, that it made her see the world as changed. Not long after she was proved right when Elvira gave up her right to inherit. I didn't see it then because I was counting on all the others and they seemed plenty to poor old me.

A cloud of memories filled every inch of every room. Gradually, all that would remain would be a pale mist, without faces or words. When the cloud dissolved into a slow rain along with my memory, a part of the life of the family would have died. The iron beds and the cheap icons above the headboards, the uneven walls and the big wooden table with two benches which would no longer wait for someone to come and sit on them. It would all get covered in dust and cobwebs until a storm opened the first crack in the walls. A little bit of the story would remain, and if one day someone remembered it and told the tale, people would listen to him with friendly, open eyes.

How time has flown, poor old man! What stories he has to tell today!

Barcelona is a house where the windows don't look onto the street. They face into the service shaft and the lift inside it.

Barcelona is everything at a set time. Before then, it's too early. After that, it's already too late. At half past seven, open the door, at eight, turn on the heating in winter, at ten give the keys to the woman who works for Flat 3, second floor, at twelve sort out the post, at nine in the evening collect the rubbish and at ten close the door again...

Barcelona is having the sky far away and the stars trembling. It is a damp sky and very grey rain.

Barcelona is not knowing anyone. Only the family. And sometimes hearing foreign words spoken. It is losing the memory of the sound of the animals at home as you look at dogs chained at dusk.

Barcelona is a small loaf of bread which is finished every day and milk from a bottle, very white, with no cream and a thin taste.

Barcelona is wordless noise and a thick silence full of memories.

It's not seeing anyone who could sympathize with me and it's seeing my grandchildren coming back from school carrying a heap of books and hearing a machine that talks and sings, and another that speaks and stares, but I never know if anyone sees me.

It is learning every day that there is very little work I can do. Sometimes washing the dishes after the meal. But who knows if they've been properly cleaned? And when Barcelona in the evening becomes a story from up north, there is no one to tell it to, and it annoys everyone that I want to turn an evening in Barcelona into some remarkable event on a forgotten mountain.

Barcelona is learning to keep quieter and quieter. Until they ask me something.

Every night in Barcelona is an adventure. It starts with a long noise from the lift and gallops through tracks and woods. It stops some place in the neighbourhood and listens to the bells. Festival peal, Rosary peal... I don't sleep until they ring the bells to announce that someone has died, and then my dreams are long conversations I can't have while awake. Often I even wake up with a smile or about to burst out laughing because of something we were just saying.

Once in a while Barcelona is someone from Pallarès who comes down to see the doctor, still carrying a whiff of cow dung or hay even though of course he cleaned himself properly. But maybe deep under the fingernails or on a strand of hair he brings the ordinary smells which make me so happy. And then I ask about everyone, about every house that remains in the village and about everything else that I can think of. When someone comes to visit, they don't interrupt me. Sometimes, they mock me a little. It is a way of being important when you know full well you have become a useless old woman.

Barcelona, for me, is something very beautiful. It is the last step before the cemetery.

Out 2010
PEIRENE TITLE NO. 1
Beside the Sea by Véronique Olmi
translated from French by Adriana Hunter

"A mesmerising portrait ... it should be read." THE GUARDIAN
....

PEIRENE TITLE NO. 2
Stone in a Landslide by Maria Barbal
translated from Catalan by Laura McGloughlin and Paul Mitchell

"... there's an understated power in Barbal's depiction of how the forces of history can shape the life of the powerless." FINANCIAL TIMES
....

PEIRENE TITLE NO. 3
Portrait of the Mother as a Young Woman
by Friedrich Christian Delius
translated from German by Jamie Bulloch

"A slim text. Huge literature." OBSERVER, VIENNA

Out 2011
PEIRENE TITLE NO. 4
Next World Novella by Matthias Politycki
translated from German by Anthea Bell

"Haunting, lyrical, wry, ironic – those are just a few of the notes struck with great originality by Matthias Politycki in his short novel."
ANTHEA BELL
....

PEIRENE TITLE NO. 5
Tomorrow Pamplona by Jan van Mersbergen
translated from Dutch by Laura Watkinson

"An intense reading experience ... Van Mersbergen tells what needs to be told and not a word more." DE MORGEN
....

PEIRENE TITLE NO. 6
Maybe This Time by Alois Hotschnig
translated from Austrian German by Tess Lewis

"He is one of the best writers of his generation."
SÜDDEUTSCHE ZEITUNG

Peirene

Contemporary European
Literature in Translation.
Thought provoking,
well designed, short.

*"Two-hour books to be
devoured in a single sitting:
literary cinema for those
fatigued by film."* TLS

Peirene's Literary Salon

Meike's Blog: The Pain and Passion
of a small Publisher

Readers' Comments

Exclusive Offers

Monthly Newsletter

www.peirenepress.com

We love to hear your comments about the books.
E-mail the publisher directly at: meike.ziervogel@peirenepress.com